CULT

A Novella

Ash Ericmore

Written by: Ash Ericmore

Copyright © 2020 Ash Ericmore

All Rights Reserved. This is a work of fiction. No part of this publication may be reproduced, distributed, or transmitted in any form or by any means, except in the case of brief quotations embodied in critical reviews.

ISBN: 9798840403631

CHAPTER 1

The building rose ominously over the fields, as the car turned from the last roundabout to the edge of the estate. From a distance, the building looked like any other shitty council tower block. It had been newly clad in what was currently considered trendy—beige tiles—but Sam knew that six months ago, when her father and she had first come to see it, it was a stock grey. Battleship, or something.

That was just after they had thrown her out of Briars Medical School. Just the thought of it made the scars on her arms tingle. She put her hand on the sleeve of her lower arm and caressed it.

But now, months on, she sat in the backseat of her parents estate car, Stone Sour pumping in her buds, and her father, Roger, and mother, Lilian, in the front. Shit piled around her like she was in storage. She pulled the wire that fed the music to her ears and both of the buds popped out, falling away. "Done it up," she said, to no one in particular.

"Looks nice," Lilian replied, watching out of the front. Sam could tell she was dubious, but she'd never seen it before.

"Newly cladded," Roger chipped in.

"Hopefully not with the same shit that lot in London had." There had been a tragic fire at a similar tower block in London a few years back and the cladding had not met fire safety standards. People had died. Lots of them.

"Language," Roger said, glancing at her in the rear view mirror.

"Bullshit," she muttered, quietly enough that neither of them heard.

They turned left, away from the opposing Tesco and into the car park of the tower block. They pulled to a stop in an empty space and just sat there. Sam was waiting for her father to give some sort of instruction as to what he expected of her, like he usually did. "Leave the stuff in the car," he said. *There it was.* "Let's go up and make a cup of tea."

Sam shrugged, and pushed the door of the car open. It stuck sometimes, but not this time, and she almost fell out onto the concrete. "Fuck's sake," she muttered, clambering straight. Her mother and father were getting out, and Sam stepped away from the car, looking first up the building. There must have been near to thirty floors. Just looking up at it made her head spin, the onset of some weird vertigo even though she hadn't left the ground. Then she dropped her eyes down to ground level and scanned the base of the mammoth building. There was some parking around the base of it—where they were—and an entrance to an underground car park over to the side that was blocked off, and looked like it had been for years. Cars were parked across the shutters as if they weren't there. Apart from that, it was a standard, shitty, council tower block from the eighties, sold off to any slumlord that wanted it, and rented out to the poor.

Being on the coast of the England, rather than in

the city, didn't make it any grander. It's not like you could smell the seaside from here. There weren't even gulls. It was a good couple of miles to the beach.

Sam circled a little, looking the building up and down before she stopped, as she saw three people over to the far side of the building. They looked young. Well, younger than her anyway, sixteen, maybe seventeen. They all had bikes they looked too big for, and were certainly too old for.

Roger stepped to her side. "Going to be friends of yours?" he asked.

Sam snorted. "I don't think so. They're just kids."

He looked at her quickly. "They don't look any younger than you."

Sam shook her head, and stepped back to the car, reaching in and retrieving her ipod and backpack, slinging it over her shoulder and pocketing the device. "Doubt," she said. That was the end of the conversation. She had spoken.

Her mother had walked away from the car clutching her handbag to her chest like she was going to be robbed. Sam knew that looking like that, she *was* likely to be robbed. She strode over to her, and pointed up at the building. "Look at it. What do you think?"

"Very nice." Lilian spoke quietly, perpetually afraid of change as always. She didn't want to be here—fuck it, none of them wanted that—but Sam and her dad at least managed to hide those thoughts and feelings. Bury them deep in the back of their minds.

"Come on." Sam sounded chipper. "Dad, you have the keys?"

He nodded, fumbling about and locking the car door.

Sam took her mum's arm and walked with her like a date. She carefully eyed the three boys who still stood, watching them. They watched as they went across the car park, and didn't move until they had gone into the building.

———

The flat was on the eighteenth floor, number one-eight-eight. The lift smelt of piss, but at least was working. It was a start. And the flat had been cleaned, if only rudimentarily. It was probably a nice flat when some architect had put pen to paper, but now it was tired. Dirty in places. And to coin the term, *unfinished*. Paper hung from the odd tear on the wall. The carpet was bare in places. Paint, chipped.

The front door was a cheap, thin wood. Unlike the oak door of the house they had moved out of, it looked like if you kicked it enough times in a pair of D.M.'s, you'd put your foot through it. And it was unpainted. Bare, dark brown wood. MDF, maybe. It led into a small hallway that ended with the living room. This flat, and likely most of the others was a corner flat, and so windows were at least aplenty. Off the hall was a door to Sam's bedroom, one to her parents, the kitchen, bathroom, and the living room at the end. When Sam and her dad came down to look at the place, three weeks ago, it was still furnished from the previous tenant who had skipped out on the tenancy, apparently. It looked more spacious currently, but they had brought a fuck ton of stuff down from the house.

Sam went over to her bedroom door and pushed it open. "Shit," she huffed. "Dad."

Roger went over and poked his nose in the door. The bed from the previous tenant was still there.

At least the rest of the room was empty.

"I'll call the agent," he said, retreating back to Lillian, and putting his arm around her.

Sam watched. He looked like he was consoling her. Perhaps he was. She went into the room and went over to the bed. She dropped to her knees and pulled the sheet up. Nothing underneath it. But up this close, there was a smell. Rancid. She got up and examined blanket discarded over the top of it. Taking a deep breath in, she pulled the blanket hard like a magician trying not to disturb any plates and glasses on a table.

The blanket came away with a flourish.

The mattress was stained black and the stench of shit burst free into the room.

"Holy fuck," she exclaimed.

Then, a movement within the black. A wiry ball of dark brown fur hidden in the glance that Sam had of the dried faeces burst out running. She screamed. She was not afraid of rats, nor was she particularly delicate, but it surprised her. The thin rodent leapt, lemming-like, from the mattress to the floor and bolted towards her.

Sam still had the blanket in her hand and she tossed it to the floor, covering the thing. It left a bump there, scurrying blinded in circles.

Her father appeared next to her. "What is it?"

Sam pointed at the blanket on the floor. And then her finger raised to the bed.

"That smell," he said.

"Fucking shit," she responded.

This time he didn't correct her language. At nineteen, she didn't want him to at the best of times, but she didn't expect that would change anytime in the next decade, at least. But this was an exceptional circumstance.

The blanket moved again.

It was Roger's turn to cry out in surprise this time. He stamped on the movement before Sam could stop him. There was a small crunch, and the movement stopped. "What was that?" he asked with a deliberate tick in his voice.

"Rat," she said, simply.

"Shit," he said, rather out of character.

The next ten minutes was spent moving the blanket with rat's corpse, the shit-laden mattress, and the bed frame for good measure, out into the corridor outside the flat. It wasn't ideal, it was hard to get by, and almost blocked the flat opposite's front door.

"No." Roger was on his cell to the letting agent. "You need to arrange it now." He curled his body around to face the wall and lowered his voice, maybe hoping that Sam and Lilian wouldn't hear. "*It smells of shit, and we put it in the corridor,*" he whispered. "Uh-huh. Yes. Well—Right." He ended the call, staring at his phone.

"Well?" Sam asked. She looked at Lilian, who had been watching her father the whole time, as she turned to the window overlooking the estate, staring out silently.

"He said that we should bring it back in if we know what's good for us, and he'll arrange someone to pick it up on Monday."

"Fuck that," Sam replied. Her father's eyes flicked from his phone to Sam and back down again without word. He may not have agreed with the language, but apparently he did, the sentiment.

"Quite."

The room soaked in silence for a few minutes, with no one speaking, and little movement. Finally, Lilian broke the quiet. "They're here," she said.

Sam's eyes widened and looked around the empty room. "But we haven't even got a TV." Roger laughed.

"The movers," Lilian continued. "They're here." She pointed out of the window, with no acknowledgement of Sam whatsoever.

CHAPTER 2

The movers loaded the bedframe into the lift as Sam watched. It was an antique bed that they said they could get up to the flat as long as it was both dismantled before they picked it up, and it fitted in the lift. They weren't going to carry it up eighteen flights of stairs.

She saw their point.

Standing in the lobby of Lanner Court, Sam was of different minds. The last piece of her bed went into the lift and the youngest of the movers made a gesture asking her if she wanted to get in and go up. She shook her head. He pushed the button and the door closed. She looked at the grime on the walls. Years of mistreatment, and zero effort in cleansing. She loved her bed, but it just didn't fit here. She looked at the mat by the entrance. It was sticky. She sighed and went out the front. The removal lorry was parked across six spaces, and they'd left one bloke sitting with his legs out the back, guarding the rest of their belongings. *Probably wise*, she thought. She glanced in the back of the lorry as she wandered by, nodding to the older man in there. To be honest if the three lads that had been there when they arrived had wanted to take something out the back, this guy wasn't going to be able to stop them.

She wandered towards the road. She could already see the supermarket on the other side of the street from the edge of the car park. Convenient, yes, but somewhat common, she thought. Coming from Camden, she was used to a residential street being a residential street. Not a busy main road, come shopping centre. At most she would have expected a church.

"Oi."

She was drawn from her thoughts by a voice. She turned, having wandered almost to the main road. Behind her were three lads with push bikes, probably the same three from earlier. She hadn't paid enough attention to what they looked like to be sure. "Yes?" she said, suddenly aware that she was a fair distance from the lorry, and the only source of a saviour from these … she looked them up and down … *boys*.

"Moving in?" The lad in the middle spoke. He had a cigarette in fingers, but it wasn't lit, he was twiddling it. His head was shaven, and his nose too big. He had piercing in his eyebrow.

"Wouldn't you like to know." Sam crossed her arms across her chest. She suddenly felt very naked out here on her own.

He nodded, looking her up and down. "You put the shitty furniture out on eighteen," he said. It wasn't a question. "I assume, that you will be takin' it back in when you've loaded your stuff into the flat." Again, not a question.

"You assume wrongly," she said. *Too brave*, she thought. *You should've just said he'd have to speak with Dad.*

"My ma lives in the flat opposite, and she can't

get out properly."

"You live in the flat opposite?" She had meant that to be her inside voice, regretting saying it immediately.

He stepped from the bike and left it drop to the ground. "Look." He took a step towards her. "I never said I lived there. I said my ma. You gonna move that fucking shit stained crap, or not?"

Sam took half a step back. "I … I don't know." She felt like her personal space had been violated.

He reached into his pocket and pulled out a blade, flicking his wrist. It was open. She couldn't take her eyes from it, stepping back once again. The blade was clean, the daylight glinted off it. He waved it upwards, drawing Sam to look at him. She obliged.

"Talk to me, cunt." He smiled and pushed his elbow into the lad on the bike next to him. He had a hoodie up, and Sam could barely see his face. "Gonna move it?"

Sam nodded. "Yes." She tried to see by him to the lorry. She could see the legs of the mover that was waiting there, but not enough of him to be able to try and get his attention. She returned her look to the boy. He smiled in a way that was neither warm, nor reassuring. Then he folded the knife away and took a step back.

For the first time Sam paid attention to the rest of him. He was wearing track suit trousers that didn't fit right. A jacket—no, a hoodie with the hood hanging down his back—and a tee underneath it. Torn. He pushed the cigarette into his mouth, but still made no attempt at lighting it. He picked up his bike. "As soon as you've finished moving shit in." He turned away and kicked himself into motion on the bike. Sam looked quickly to the other two. The one he'd elbowed was younger, maybe. The other had a baseball hat on. He looked about the same age. They all looked a little younger than Sam. But they were as big, tall, and the one in the baseball hat was stockier. The other two turned circles on the bike and rode away, following the first.

"Fucking shit," Sam muttered under her breath. She waited for them to pass the lorry and get a way by the tower block, before she started to follow. When she got up level with the removal lorry, the mover nodded at her, making some sort of jovial acknowledgement. He'd seen nothing, but Sam just shook her head and continued back to the building. She went in and started up the stairs.

CHAPTER 3

There was shouting coming from down the corridor. Sam stood in the doorway of the stairwell. She'd taken her time coming up *eighteen fucking flights* of stairs, but it had allowed her to have a toke on the joint she had in her back pocket. She had wondered if she was going to find a new dealer coming down here. She didn't smoke much, but she preferred to score her own rather than bumming it off anyone, and she wasn't going to know anyone, anyway.

However, if the graffiti on the walls of the stairwell were correct, she could get the number of at least two dealers from there, and also *Fat Peter* who liked to *Gape Arseholes*. Also, she could probably ask that nice lad with the bike and knife. He probably knew someone.

"Fuck off."

The voice brought her back to the here and now. It was one of the movers. She looked around the corner. Two big guys were up in the face of one of the movers, and there was broken glass on the floor. Sam could see her dad standing in the doorway of the flat blocking movement either in or out. He had his phone in his hand, nervous. *Oh great,* she thought, *he's going to call the police on our new neighbours.* That stupid dickwad from downstairs may have been pushing his luck but she wasn't going to get shanked over a fucking mattress. Not today, and not tomorrow. She'd just move the fucking thing regardless of what her dad had to say, throw it out the window if necessary, and maybe ingratiate herself with the locals. It was clear even now that it was one of *those* estates, and she'd rather not spend the next six months looking over her shoulder.

Six months.

That was how long they had taken a tenancy for, and how long her father had promised it would take for him to get back on his feet.

Fuck it. She left the corner and started towards the argument in the corridor. The two men that were facing down the mover were older than she was. Twenties, maybe. At least they weren't boys. It appeared the argument was about something that had been knocked from the movers hands by one of the other men. Now they seemed to be threatening to push the movers face into the shit strained mattress. Sam stopped in the centre of the corridor and waited. There was no way around them to the front door, and she wasn't about to interrupt.

The shorter of the two men took a step back, weighing up the mover. "I will erase you from the memories of your cunt children," he said.

Interesting insult, Sam thought. The mover didn't speak. He was glued to the spot, looking like he was going to shit at any moment.

"Huh," the shorter guy said, and pushed the mover's shoulder.

The mover went against type, and didn't move.

"Huh," he said, again, but before the shove

landed this time, two more movers came by her father, and filled the corridor. *The heavy lifters.*

The heavy lifters seemed to diffuse the situation quickly. The shorter guy and his friend immediately backed off.

"Problem?" asked the bigger lifter of the two. He had a deep voice, far deeper than it should have been for a ginger. Size of a brick shithouse, though. He looked at the mover they threatened. "Bruv?"

That seemed to end it right there. The two guys—presumably from the block—backed further away, crushing the broken glass under foot. "Yeah," the shorter one said, as they turned to pass Sam, heading towards the lift and stairwell. He looked her down quickly. "Nice tits," he said.

Sam raised an eyebrow. *They are, yes, but you'll never know.*

They stomped off, rounding the corner, and were gone. There was patting of shoulders and a little consolation play amid the movers, but with the situation over, everyone moved on.

Except Sam.

She watched her father return into the flat, to her mother, to move furniture about, and she watched the movers go down the corridor to return with their last loads of belongings.

Within an hour they were done, and the family were finally in.

Sam looked at the shit stained mattress still

leaning against the corridor outside the door. She pulled her marigolds on and dragged the thing into the flat.

"What on earth …?" Roger stood in the doorway of the living room, hunched over the sofa he was dragging from one side of the room to the other.

"They said that there would be trouble if we didn't keep it in here until it was picked up."

He stood, arching his back and pushing his hand into his spine. "You can't let people push you around, love," he said. "That's not our problem."

She pulled it across the corridor and into her bedroom door. "No, it's not our problem. It's mine."

CHAPTER 4

With the windows wide open the stench of shit subsided into a foul odour, and then to a mild inconvenience quite quickly. Despite her father's objection that the mattress should, under no circumstance, be kept in her bedroom, that was where it was going to be kept. The blanket plus squish rat had gone down the rubbish shoot. She had dismantled the bedframe and stood it up against the wall in front of some vent that fed out into the wall. Creepy looking thing. Probably some nineteen sixties attempt at air-con.

Sam sat on her bed, staring out of the window to the sun setting over Tesco. Even here, in this shit stained, arse-gaping, joyless tenement, the sunset was still pretty. She pulled a tee over her head, one that didn't even come close to matching the shorts she was wearing. But who cared? She was in for the night.

Sam's feeling of serenity was broken by a scream. It wasn't loud, but they were on the eighteenth, and it was coming from out the window. She hurried over and looked out, down the sheer drop to the car park. There was no one down there but the height made her dizzy, the view flexing in her head. It made her want to puke.

"Please, no!"

It was coming from above. Sam twisted around and two storey's up and a couple of windows over, a torso was half hanging out, headfirst. Arms dangling.

"Fucking hell," Sam said. She pulled herself clear of the window and ran across the room out in the hallway of the flat.

"Dinner's nearly ready," her mum said as Sam bolted towards the front door.

"I won't be long." Sam slammed the front door behind her and ran for the stairs. No time to wait for the lift. She already found that it could take five minutes or more to reach you. She hit the stairwell, and went up.

Two floors.

She burst out from the stairs and into the corridor. There was another scream. Why was no one else coming to help? She heard voices coming from an open door along the corridor and she went for it.

"Where is Noah?" the voice asked. Sam recognised it as the voice of the shorter of the two from the corridor earlier.

"I don't fucking know, Leo. Fucking pull me in."

Sam got to the door and looked in. It was a different layout to hers, the front door of the flat was in the middle of the living room. Leo, and the other guy from earlier were standing by the window, hanging on to a pair of legs. "Fucking hell," she blurted.

Leo turned, saw her and smiled. "Oi, oi, Jez. Looksy here. It's Nice Tits." Jez turned to look, the two of them holding firmly on to squirming legs.

They turned back to face each other, and gave some sort of nod of agreement, and then hoisted the man from the window.

His scream died almost instantly as he dropped away, plummeting the twenty floors.

Sam went cold.

"Get her," said Leo.

Sam turned and ran toward the stairs. They were big lads, probably slow. At least, that *might* be the thing that saved her. She shouldered through the door and started upwards. There was no sense in pulling her mum and dad into this, and going down the stairs would surely do that. She wanted to lead them away, and find a way down after she had gotten a distance from them. She had the whole building to try.

She was on the next floor before they followed through the door. She heard muffled instructions, and she carried on, hearing them follow. They were slow on the stairs. She carried on a few more flights, and then out into a corridor. Floor 24, the sign said.

Panicked, she didn't know what to do. Bang on doors? Scream rape? Run? Hide? It nagged at the back of her mind that no one else had come to help the bloke in the window. She turned down the corridor and ran, hard. There was a door at the other end. A fire escape. Alarmed. Sure to be. That didn't sound too bad. Alarms going off? People thinking the building was on fire? Maybe, just maybe, leaving their fucking homes.

Her feet pounded on the floor and as she got

within reaching distance of the door, she saw the chain wrapped around it. She crashed, full speed into it and screamed, "*You lousy mother fucker.*"

And the door to her left opened. Flat 247.

An elderly woman pushed her face out into the hallway. A sweet looking octogenarian. "Problem?" she asked.

Sam sucked air in, giving a quick look back the way she had come. "Do you mind?" she asked, almost pushing the woman aside.

"Not at all," she replied, moving out the way.

Sam went into her flat, and across the living room. The flat smelt of old people. She walked straight to the window and pushed her face against the glass. She couldn't see the base of the building, not even close, and she banged the palm of her hand on the window out of desperation. "No," she muttered.

"What's the problem, dear?" The old woman had followed her to the window and looked out, trying to see what Sam was looking for.

"They dropped someone out the window."

The woman looked at her. "Oh, I doubt that. Probably a prank. Cuppa tea?"

Sam stared out to the dusky sky and nodded. Maybe she was right. Maybe it was all a fucking joke. She turned back as the woman shuffled across the room and out into a pokey hall off the living room. She went and sat on the sofa and held her head in her hands, listening as the old woman rattled cups and saucers, a teapot.

She also kept one ear on the front door. Almost waiting for Leo and Jez to open it and walk in.

The old woman returned without the front door being opened. She placed a tray on the poof at the end of the sofa with two cups of pissy looking tea, and a saucer covered in bourbons, on it.

She passed one of the cups to Sam and rested the saucer on the arm of the sofa, before retiring to the armchair across from Sam. "So you're the new family, just moved in?" she asked.

Sam stiffened.

Seeing her reaction the old woman smiled. "No need to worry about me, my dear. Word gets around is all. I'm Jenny, but most people around here call me Nanny." Again the warm smile.

Sam sipped her tea. It tasted pissy too. "Nice to meet you, Nanny. I'm Sam. So have you lived here long?"

Nanny bobbed her head and Sam didn't know if it was a voluntary reaction or not. "Oh, yes. One of the first, me."

Sam nodded. She wasn't overly comfortable with the situation, but better this than the alternative. "We're down from London," she continued. It was warm in here. Too fucking warm. *Old person warm*.

"I know, my dear. You and your la-di-da furniture, and your fancy ornaments. Fucking wankers."

Sam looked at her. "What?"

"London bankers, was it? Your dad, I mean. What does he do?"

Sam blinked a couple of times. It was getting hotter. "Do you mind if I get some air?" She motioned to the window.

"I think you should stay right there." Nanny stood and shuffled over to Sam, taking the cup from her hand. "Don't you fucking dare stain my sofa."

Sam was tired. Hot. Her stomach bubbled like she was going to throw up. Or shit. Both. She watched Nanny walk around the sofa and go towards the front door. "What have you done?" The last word barely came out. She slumped back, still able to make out Nanny at the door. She opened it. Leo was on the other side. They exchanged words, but it was getting harder for Sam to hear.

Everything was going dark.

CHAPTER 5

Sam's head hurt. She struggled to open her eyes. They hurt. The actual balls of her eyes stung as she tried to open them. Even as she blinked it away and fought for her eyes to adjust to the light. It was dark, and one eye was adjusting quicker than the other, disorienting her further. She wanted to wipe her face with her hand, but she couldn't. Sickness rose and fell in her.

What was going on?

She squinted. She couldn't see anything. There was something over her face. What the fuck? She tried to move again. Something held her hands. Ropes, something. She was tied down, onto something hard, and flat. She couldn't move her feet either. "What the fuck?" She spoke the words this time, but they came out wrong, broken. She could feel something in her mouth with her tongue. Something smooth *in* her mouth, stopping her from speaking.

She panicked and fought against the binds, shaking her head from side to side to try and dislodge whatever covered her. Nothing seemed to do any good. She was still tied tight, her face covered, her mouth gagged.

And then a man's voice from next to her head quietly said, "Now, now, little girl. Calm your furs."

Sam tried to scream, but for all the energy she spent, all she achieved was making her throat sore.

Then she felt skin on her leg, just above the knee. She wailed again, inside the gag, and tried to flinch away, squirming to move. Trapped.

He laughed.

Sam felt movement. She was being wheeled on something. A bang, and a lurch. She was wheeled *into* something. And then she felt it. She was being pushed through a door like she was on a gurney in the hospital. Her stomach turned with fear. She could hear people laughing. There was cheering, and it was getting louder. She fought against the binds, kicking out her legs and arms. She could feel them digging into her, cutting against her skin. She could feel the warmth of blood as it let lightly from her wrists.

And the crowd became so loud it was deafening.

"What have we here then?"

"Fresh fucking meat."

Sam could only hear some of the jibes against her over the crowd, most of whom didn't seem to be aiming much at her, directly. She felt like she was being wheeled into the back of an event, a fucking wrestling match, or something. Something wet hit her legs, something *splashed* on her. She tried to cry out, she tried to call out for her father, but no words passed the gag.

The gurney banged as it rode over something. Clunking like a car on speedbumps. The voices echoed around the space, bouncing back and forth from the walls. She could barely make out anything that was being said, called, shouted.

Then the room started to fall to a hush. Close to her, at first. They stopped, and then those near them stopped, and finally the room was all but silent.

Sam could hear the sound of her own breathing. She could hear someone crying, but it sounded so far away, and she could hear struggling. Struggling that sounded no different to her own. Then the gurney stopped and the room fell silent, besides the weeping of a woman.

CHAPTER 6

"Good evening."

The thick burlap that was hooded over Sam's face was roughly pulled from it. She was blinded by the sudden intrusion of light and quickly tried to blink it away. She was facing a hard grey concrete ceiling. Her senses suddenly flooded over her when her sight returned. She was cold. Cool air ran over her. She knew she wasn't, but she felt naked. She could smell sweat. Grease. Dirt. She lifted her head. She was still wearing the clothes she had on before, thank fuck. Tee and shorts.

She looked around for the first time.

There were men standing, watching her.

She couldn't see how many to count. But they stood over her, threatening. The looks on their faces suggested that the sight of a nineteen-year-old girl tied to a gurney was neither a shock, nor unwanted. She made the mistake of looking into the eyes of one of them. She'd seen the look before. When she was in school, fifteen years old, one of the sub-teachers had looked at her like that. He'd spent the day too close to her, brushing against her. He was a dirty fucking pervert, stopped only by the system. She'd known then that if he had his way, he would have fucked her. And this guy was the same.

Difference was, this time she was tied to a fucking gurney and surrounded by fucking psychos.

No system in place. Nothing to protect her.

As sudden as it came, the fight in Sam subsided. She was overtaken by a horrid, vile, fear. So strong, it almost blinded her.

"Let her through," the voice came again. It was a woman. Sam knew the voice.

The gurney started moving again. Rumbling her forward. For every inch she moved through the crowd, she tensed harder. It made her sore on the hard gurney.

She looked back to the ceiling, stealing her eyes from seeing into anyone else's. Shit electric lights hung from chains on the ceiling. She saw words painted on the concrete as they passed stanchions. The words were yellow, but faded. *Exit*. As she cleared the edge of the crowd, she saw the woman stood atop a small constructed stage.

Nanny.

She sucked in a sharp breath and braved looking around again. There was Nanny and there was someone else on the stage, tied maybe, but onto a contraption, not a gurney like she was. Also with the head covered. Sam looked into the crowd. They looked … wanton. Evil. But most frighteningly, they looked at her with desire. Men, she noticed. They were all men. Her head flicked from side to side as she tried to see a way out, she pulled at the binds. She thrashed her head trying to loosen the gag. There was a sea of them. Maybe thirty? More?

Fuck.

Then there was a clunk as something vibrated through the gurney, and Sam was raised from horizontal to vertical. She slipped a few inches as weigh shifted and her binds held her in place.

The crowd let out a roar as she was brought to a standing position. She watched them leering at her body, craving her. Then Nanny called for quiet. The room hushed, the echo's stopped. Still, there was a quiet weeping.

Nanny stepped with quiet calm to the edge of the stage. "Welcome, my daughter." She smiled.

Sam tried to respond. To tell her to go fuck herself, but the gag stopped the words, letting out only muffled grunts.

"I'll make her grunt," came a voice from the crowd. There was a low ripple of laughter, and someone even clapped.

Nanny waved her hands in a downward, hushing motion. "Calm down, boys," she said. "You'll get your turn."

Sam wanted to vomit.

"Welcome." She looked at Sam. "Welcome to the Court of Lanner."

The crowd cheered. It was like their sports team had just won at sports. *Fucking cunts.* Sam wildly looked around.

"I suppose I should do some sort of induction before we begin," Nanny said. Another short ripple of applause. "The Lanners are responsible for the cleansing of the bloodline, and you, my dear, are now one of us." She gestured towards Sam. "You can be as happy as you like in your new position." She stopped for a second, before delivering the punchline. "Or positions." They all laughed. "But regardless, you will be required to produce girl babies. We have not been lucky in the last two generations. Siblings don't make great babies."

"But we like trying." The same voice from the crowd. A longer, lower, laugh, and the slapping sound of some high fives.

"Quite," said Nanny. "Get me Neil."

There was some pushing and shoving in the crowd as they acted with some strange level of boisterousness. It was all playful, like this didn't mean … anything. Then, ejected from the crowd came *Neil*. It was the boy with the bike that Sam had a run in with this morning. *Shit.*

He looked at her wearing a shit-eating grin, fist-pumping, and bumping, and generally bro-ing down like he was about to make a pass at some chick in a pub. Bravado. They were cheering him on, making him feel like he was the man. *A* man.

"Come on, young man," Nanny said, waving him towards the stage. There was that word again. *Man.*

It made Sam feel sick. This boy wasn't a fucking real man. She pulled her wrists hard. She could see blood weeping from the cuts that were being made by the cable-ties. She wasn't getting out by pulling. She looked down to her feet. Same. Wrapped around her ankles, and smattered in blood.

Neil climbed up onto the stage. He was bouncing, his hands in the air, like a boxer, winning, jeering his opponent. The crowd had risen to a dull roar of support in whatever endeavour this cunt was about partake in. And the thought of what that was made Sam feel like she was going to puke.

They were going to rape her. That much was obvious. But *he* was going to do it now.

Nanny waved the crowd quiet again.

There was that sound. Again. Weeping.

"Bring her forward." Nanny took Neil by the shoulder and led him across the stage to the side, and the other person, under burlap, was wheeled to the centre of the stage. They were on their feet. Sam could see their feet under the burlap walking as best they could, as two man dragged whatever it was under there.

When they stopped, Nanny gave them the nod, and they pulled back the burlap, letting it drop to the floor.

It was her mother.

Sam screamed, audibly, even through the gag, and she felt the skin from her throat flare as she did.

Lilian was head down in medieval stocks. A pillory framework, with holes for the wrists and head. An instrument of torture and humiliation. She was wearing a blindfold under the burlap, and a ball-gag. She was wearing the same dress that she wore when

Sam had left the flat to go looking for the people upstairs. Whenever that was. Earlier today, probably. It was the red dress that her dad liked. It wasn't particularly revealing, but rather classy. Like *they* were. She pulled so hard against the cable-ties, she felt the plastic digging down to her bones. Her back arched from the gurney, and she convulsed her whole body back and forth like she was having an epileptic fit, trying to get free, trying to break something.

And where was her father?

A man—she paid him no attention at all—came around from the side of her, and slammed his fist into her gut. Sam stopped convulsing, and dropped limply against the binds, her knees falling away weakly from under her. She wanted to puke, but it hurt to breathe in, allowing her only the most shallow of breaths before pain stabbed at her, making her stop.

Sam couldn't move now. Not with any sense of purpose, anyway.

Nanny walked across the stage to Sam's mum, and pulled the blindfold from her. She looked around bucking against the stocks. Then her eyes landed on Sam and she tried to scream against the ball-gag, with nothing more than a muffle coming out. "A family reunion, of sorts," Nanny said. "And you, Neil, want to be part of the family?"

Neil pumped his hand up in the air and pulled off his shirt revealing his thin emaciated body beneath. He threw it out in the crowd like he was some sort of stripper.

Again, Nanny waved the crowd to a hush. She looked over to Sam. "What do you think honey?" she asked. "How about Neil be your new father?"

Sam tried to pull herself up, but in vain. Her mother was crying. She was watching Nanny, and Neil. Neil turned. He looked at Lilian. Walked over and bent down so that his face was at the same height as hers. He slapped her, gently, on the cheek.

The crowd watched, hushed.

Nanny said, "Do you want to fuck?" She waved her hands up this time, riling the crowd. "Need some practice? This one's no good for anything else!"

Neil bounced again, hands up. "Yeah," he shouted over and over again.

He went to the side of the stage and came back with a blade. Sam couldn't see what it was exactly, but it was large—like a butcher's knife, or a cleaver. Neil went over to her mum and showed her the blade, making her cry out more, teasing her with it, Lilian unable to take her eyes from it.

The crowd lowered their cheers, becoming more jokey with each other, letting Neil do as he wanted, take his time. Let him *feel* his way. He rounded her and slapped her on the arse with the flat of the blade. She tried to move. She tried to scream. Neil crouched down used the knife to cut her dress up the back revealing her underwear. He laughed. Pinged them like he was on the school playground. He grinded against her like they were on a dance floor.

All the while he had that shit-eating grin on his

face, enjoying every second of it.

He cut her underwear from her.

Lilian tried to shake her way from his grip but it was no good. He pushed himself against her, simulating fucking her. He laughed, his head back. Then he raised the knife and started making a chopping motion that brought the crowd back. They started cheering, and then a chant. *Fuck the bitch. Fuck the bitch. Fuck the bitch.* Over and over. Neil bent forward and placed the blade down on the stage directly below Lilian's face. Just so she could see it. So she could be scared of it.

He unbuttoned his jeans and pulled them down. Even through his pants, Sam could see he was hard.

Sam was starting to feel weak. It was like her blood wasn't flowing to her head, and she was getting faint. It made it all seem somehow dream like.

Neil dropped his pants and the crowd went apeshit. The roar was deafening, and did nothing more than add to the confusion that Sam felt.

He waved his hard cock in her mum's face, as she pulled away as far as she could. He slapped her cheek with it. The crowd were loving it.

Then he picked up the blade again. While he was down there, he said something to her, lost to the noise of the crowd.

Then he stood.

He used his free hand to unbuckle the ball-gag from her mum, and let it drop to the ground, holding on to the blade with the other.

She mouthed, *I love you*, to Sam and, nodded some sort of *It'll be okay*.

It wasn't going to be okay. It was already too late to be okay. Sam tried to mouth words back, but she couldn't close her lips, her own gag, deep in her mouth.

Neil waved the blade again and started to circle her mum. Naked. Hard.

Fucking animal cunt.

The Neil stopped, facing Sam. He waved the blade in her direction and said something but she couldn't hear what. It was probably a promise of similar to come to her. Then he turned back to her mum. He raised the blade, and hacked it down hard on the back of her mum's neck. The blade stopped violently as it tore between the vertebrae. Her mum went limp as blood gushed from the wound. Neil tried to lift the blade out, but it was struck fast in her neck. He raised his leg and leant it against the stocks.

He was still hard.

He used the extra leverage to pull the blade out, blood splattering his naked torso, splashing against his cock. On his face. Down his legs.

Sam couldn't look away.

He brought it up again, and the crowd's excitement rose. The blade slid through her mum's neck this time, free of the bone, and her head dropped to the stage in front of her.

Blood gushed out of her neck like it had been pent up. Then it evened to a flow as the pressure dropped. As the heart stopped. Neil slung the blade across the stage, it clattering on the floor.

He turned, and inserted his cock into Sam's mum's gaping neck. And he fucked her lifeless corpse, his bloody arsehole facing her, as the crowd cheered.

Sam heard Nanny ask the crowd something. She couldn't hear or wasn't listening. It didn't matter now. This had … this. The words, the thoughts weren't there.

Someone from the crowd got up on the stage and came around behind her mum. He dropped his trousers and although she couldn't see, she knew he was fucking her too.

Sam felt vomit rise in her stomach, pushing itself into her mouth. The taste of burning was vile and she tried to swallow it back, but she felt it seeping around the edge of the gag. Out onto her chin. Dripping down onto her body.

"Winner takes it all," Nanny shouted above the crowd.

Neil and the other cunt had a rhythm now, fucking spit-roasting her dead mother, until Neil pulled away first. She couldn't see amid the gore and the blood, and bits of hacked off flesh, *she didn't want to see*, but she assumed that Neil had cum first.

The crowd approved.

Sam couldn't hold her head up anymore. She

slumped forward, held up by her binds, and closed her eyes.

CHAPTER 7

Sam awoke looking at her father. They were back in the flat. Roger was sitting on one of their dining chairs looking at her. He had the gag this time. He was tied, his feet to the legs, his hands at the wrist to the arms of the chair, and he was naked.

Sam looked down at herself.

She was naked too.

Tied the same as he was to another chair. But no gag. She ran her tongue around the inside of her mouth. She could feel a chipped tooth where the last gag had been forced into her while she was unconscious. She could taste the odious filth of bile in her mouth.

She strained to look around. They were in the living room. "Where are they?" she asked.

Her father shook his head. He made some effort to talk, but he couldn't.

Then she remembered everything. It came flooding back and hit her like a shovel to the face. "Mum," she said with a sharp intake of breath.

Roger lowered his head. He already knew. She just hoped for his sake that he didn't see it.

Behind her, the toilet flushed, and the door to the bathroom opened. A man came out, tugging on his fly. "Fucking jeans," he said. "Get what you pay for." He was bald, and tanned—badly, with an itchy looking red patch disappearing from his neck into the v of his shirt. An earring in one ear. He walked in, between Sam and Roger, and looked from him to her. His eyes lingered on Sam's body and he nodded some sort of approval. "Nice."

Sam rolled the saliva in her throat up to her mouth and spat at him, gob reaching the bottom of his jeans.

"Save it for later, love." He turned back to her father and walked around, behind him. He leaned down onto her dad's shoulder's, looking at Sam over the top of his head, with his arms draped on Roger. "Good looking girl, you got there, old man. *Spunky.*" He grinned at Sam chewing on some invisible gum. "But," he continued. "We need to see if this is all going to work out."

"What the fuck's going on?" Sam screamed at him.

He raised an eyebrow. "Now, now." He stood and took hold of Roger's shoulders, massaging him like a prize-fighter waiting in the corner of the ring.

Her dad snapped his head back and forth trying to see what he was doing.

"I'm Peter, by the way. And I am here to establish whether you …" He slapped his hands down on Roger's bare shoulders. "… are going to be any good to us."

Sam's father made muffled protests through the gag.

"I know, I know." He walked around to his side

and crouched, resting his hand on roger's knee. "You see, we need new stock. And we haven't been having much luck with that in the last few years." He stood. "And our Nanny, bless her, decided that your little girl here is going to be our saviour. However …" He turned to face him. "… that means that you are going to have to do your bit too. Join the cause, so to speak. Do you understand?"

Sam watched as her father stared straight into the man's eyes. He shook his head. Slightly.

Peter turned to face Sam. "I don't think you understand," he said, quietly. "That said, though, I do stand to lose a fiver if you so much as get a hard-on for your little girl." Peter then walked from between the two of them and crossed the living room, going out into the corridor.

Sam's father stared at her. He shook his head, and was crying now. He made no movement, no sound, but he wept.

"Dad …" She didn't want to say the words, but she had to. "You've got to. They're going to …" Her voice drifted off as she thought of the depravity her mother faced. "They'll hurt you."

He shook his head.

"Dad. You must."

Peter came back into the room. He wasn't alone. Two other blokes were with him, around the same height, build, a little younger maybe. "Right. Me and the boys here are ready for the show. No privacy in this tribe, mate. Up you get."

Roger looked at Peter for a moment, his head shook from side to side slowly.

Peter met his shaking with nodding, and when nothing changed, he simply said, "Hold on." He walked back out of the room, returning only a few seconds later with a set of rusty old garden shears, the sort used to trim hedges. "If you can't get hard for your little girl, then you are no good to us." He punctuated the sentence by snapping the shears closed a couple of times. "I will cut your cock off and feed it to your little girl while you watch, geddit?" He snapped the shears again.

"Dad," Sam interrupted.

Roger looked at her.

"Focus. Close your eyes. Think of mum. Think of whatever you have to."

He shook his head as he pissed himself.

"Then look at me," she said. "Pretend I'm someone else. Someone you want to fuck." She looked at Peter. He was starting to get agitated. Impatient. He was staring at her father, caring little to nothing about her. "Come on," she continued. "You want to have it," she said desperately. She pulled her legs open at the knees as far as they would go. "Fuck my cunt." She said. "Fuck me like a whore."

Still he protested, sitting in his own piss, his body jiggling as he cried harder, muted by the gag.

Sam looked at Peter. He was closer to her father. He'd moved. He wanted to win his fiver. He wanted to end this charade. Sam glanced at his friends. Both of them were paying her more attention than anything else in the room, getting turned on by her actions. She returned her attention to her father. He had his head dropped down onto his chest.

"Oh dear, oh dear, oh dear." Peter reached the side of the chair. "Don't want to fuck your little girl, do you?"

He shook his head, silently.

Peter looked at Sam. "Don't take it personally," he said. "These two want to fuck you. I think that Neil's *going* to fuck you. Most everybody is *actually* going to fuck you. It's just this dried up old cunt that doesn't want to."

"Fuck off, you—" Words failed her. She looked at her father again. "Dad," she said quietly.

"Sorry, old man," Peter said. He opened the shears just a little and slid them down into Roger's crotch. Sam was grateful that they weren't closer and that she'd be able to see more. She didn't want to see more.

Then Peter snapped the shears closed.

After a second of silence, Sam's father began to scream so loudly it rounded the ball-gag and could probably have been heard in the flat above. Blood erupted from between his legs, mixing with the piss at first and then overtaking it, dripping from the chair to the carpet, trickling down his legs. He bit down on the gag so hard, his front teeth cracked, and one split in half, splitting his gum and causing a torrent of blood from his mouth.

"Yee-haw," Peter cawed. He reached down into Sam's father's lap and lifted his blood soaked, flaccid penis up like a dirty rag. "Cock-tastic," he said, laughing.

Sam looked down at herself, suddenly aware of her nakedness, and that she was still holding her knees open for her father. She closed them. Snapped them shut. Peter cackled. One of the other two let out a disappointed grunt. Sam couldn't stop herself from glancing in his direction.

She half expected to catch him having a wank.

Thankfully he wasn't, but he saw her look and thrust his pelvis at her.

Her father still screamed. It filled the room.

"Shut the fuck up, old man," screamed Peter at him. "It's not like you were using it." He tossed his penis to the carpet, only just shy of Sam's feet, causing her to recoil in disgust. She edged her toes as far away as the binds that held her to the chair would allow. Peter punched Sam's father, and he stopped screaming, his head jolting to the side and dropping. The pool of blood crawling across the carpet was vast. He had lost so much blood he was going pale.

"What do you want?" Sam managed to say. She was fighting her whole body's desire to black out again. Sickness sat in her stomach. Her head swam.

"Right," Peter said. He straightened himself and passed the shears to his friends. One of them left the room with them and the other shook Peter's hand, nodding some shitty congratulatory wank at him like he'd just scored big in snooker. He turned to Sam's father and stood over him. He wasn't a big man, in either sense of the word. He was average height and a cunty waste of skin. But her father had never looked so small.

Peter took him by the chin and rolled his head around, admiring his face. Then he rested his head back and pulled his fist back. He punched him on the chin. Her father rocked in the chair, still unconscious. Peter did it again. There was a crack. A crunch. More teeth on the ball-gag Sam suspected.

She still fought to stay awake. She knew well enough what they had in store for her, but the last thing she could think of right now was waking up to find they'd already done it—or worse, that they were doing it there and then.

Peter punched him in the throat. A gurgle. Blood was rushing down her father's chin, onto his chest, his stomach, mixing with the congealing blood already on the chair. The carpet. He suddenly seemed to wake. He started coughing up the blood that was running down his throat. Choking.

Peter laughed, and stepped away. "This fucker's drowning in his own blood." He turned to Sam. "Daddy's little girl want a real man?"

"Fuck you," she said, not taking her eyes off her dad. Peter was right, she feared. He was barely conscious and drowning in his own blood. What of it that was left inside his body, that is.

Peter turned back to her father and lifted his face

up again. He didn't even look at Peter, his eyes rolled in is head. He was no longer aware of his surroundings. He wasn't *really* awake. "Cunt," Peter said under his breath. He looked at Sam. "Don't go anywhere will you?" He laughed. His friend laughed.

They walked out of sight from the living room and Sam listened as the front door closed. She waited a few seconds. There was no sound at all. They'd left.

CHAPTER 8

Sam writhed in the chair trying to get loose. "Stay with me, dad," she kept saying. He'd stopped moving a few minutes ago. She didn't know how long she had before Peter came back. Probably with Neil. The ropes she fought against now dug into the cuts she had from the cable ties on the gurney. It split them open. They bled fresh. "Fucking hell." She tried kicking out. Break the chair. Something. Anything.

There was a crash from outside the living room. They were coming and Sam was still just as tied as she was. *I'm fucked*, she thought. *Literally*.

She still pulled against the ropes but it was doing no good. She didn't take her eyes from the doorway, waiting to see who was coming first.

There was some movement, and a slight, scrawny young man stuck his head around the door. He looked at Sam's father. "Holy shit," he whispered. Then he saw Sam staring at him. "*Holy shiiiiiit.*" He came into the room. He was dirty. Tee and jeans that didn't look like he'd changed them in a month. Hair was straggled, unkempt. He had dirt on his face. He was carrying a backpack and a hunting knife.

"Who the fuck are you?" Sam asked.

"Noah," he whispered. "Keep your fucking voice down." He dropped down next to her and started to cut away the ropes on her feet. "Let's get you out of here. Before they come back." He couldn't stop himself from glancing at her body. As soon as he'd cut Sam free from the ropes she stumbled across the room to her father, bloody and ruined. She didn't know what to touch, pawing at him softly, tears streaming down her face.

"He's done for," said Noah. "Come on, before they come back."

"I love you, dad," she whispered. She turned as Noah was leaving the living room, but instead of going for the front door he hooked a right into Sam's bedroom. She followed.

Noah was in the room piling bits of bed up that he had knocked over when he'd climbed out of the vent in her room. "Get in. Quick."

Sam grabbed the sweatshirt and shorts that were on the bed and threw them into the vent, crawling in naked, after them.

Noah crawled in backwards, covering the vent with pieces of the bed, and re-securing the vent cover. "Mind the drop in the dark," he said. "There's a ladder to the next floor. We'll talk there."

Sam pulled her clothes on before feeling carefully for the ladder. "How big is the drop?"

"Only about four metres."

Only. Sam found the rungs and worked her way down.

———

The hatch into the vent was only just over a foot square. It had been a struggle for her to get in, but the vents themselves were larger, and allowed some rudimentary free movement. On the floor below, Noah reached the bottom of the ladder and overtook Sam. "Follow me," he whispered. "Keep your voice down while we are out here."

Sam followed him through the labyrinthine system of vents for a few minutes without word. She just wanted to keep moving forward and not think about the past.

Noah stopped and turned at a corner. He gestured for Sam to follow and he disappeared around. When Sam turned the corner she found herself in a small enclosure. A room just big enough for two adults to sleep in.

"Welcome to my abode," he said, speaking normally. He waved for her to sit. "Make yourself at home." He nodded at the walls, a gentle humming coming through them. "Best I can work out, this is the heart of the old central air. The motors still function, but it's been shagged for years. Thankfully, the motors keep the noise out and vice versa. So they can't hear us in here." He stuck his hand out and Sam shook it. "So, yeah, Noah. You are?"

"Sam. I think someone was looking for you." She remembered the guy that was being dangled out the window.

"I suspect so." He grinned. Then he rummaged around in the stuff on the floor. It was clear he was living here. There was a dirty sleeping bag pushed up against the wall, and tins, packets, leftover food stuffs. He retrieved an open can of baked beans, fork sticking out the top. He offered it to her.

Sam shook her head.

He shrugged and started to eat.

"So," Sam wasn't sure what to ask first, so the words trailed off, and she started to cry. The tears flooded forward and she held her head in her hands.

Noah watched on, wordless.

After a few minutes the tears stopped. There were none left. She didn't want to stop, but her body couldn't make anymore. She slumped against the wall of the room, exhausted. "Talk to me," she said. "Who are you? What's going on?"

Noah sat back and put the bean can down. "Noah Miles. Occupant of Flat One Eight Eight, Lanner Court." He looked at her and smiled. "You stole my flat. I moved in in March, when the weather was bad, and I moved into the air vents in April. Been here ever since."

"Why haven't you left?"

"I can't. You'll see. The corridors are all on CCTV. These vents don't go as far as the edge of the building anywhere. I've tried to steal a phone and call for help." He picked a mobile phone from the clutter and tossed it to her. "Eight figure numerical password. And that's not the first one I've tried, either. They know I'm in here, I think. At least they know I'm in the building somewhere. Spanner in the works. They just can't find me."

"I saw them drop someone out the window on one of the higher floors. They were asking for you."

Noah looked sad. "Well. It's not like I had any mates here, so I don't know who they could have been asking."

Sam closed her eyes. "Who are they?"

"The Court of Lanner. Yes. Well. When I moved in, like you, I guess, I had no idea. They left me alone longer than you, by the look of it. As soon as you moved in your stuff I was watching from the vent in my—your—," he corrected himself, "—bedroom. As far as I can gather they're a bunch of inbreds. It's like a shit horror movie, except instead of being in a Louisiana swamp, we're in a fucked up block of flats in England. Nanny runs the place. There's a couple of higher level thugs, Fat Peter's the worst. Rapist cunt." He looked at Sam. "So what happened to your Mum?"

Sam looked at him. The tears had dried now. "They cut her in half and fucked the bits."

"I'm sorry," he said. "I really am. At least I was alone. They tried to indoctrinate me into all this and I panicked. I think climbing in here was the only thing that's kept me alive."

Sam started to look around the floor. "You have any weapons?"

"I've got this." He tapped the knife on his belt. "Found it one of the flats. I don't know if anyone has missed it yet. Aside from that, not really. Why? You looking to find a way out—like I said, it's not possible."

"No," she replied quiet calmly. "Finding a way out is a by-product. It's an aside. What I'm going to do is kill every mother-fucking one of the cunts."

CHAPTER 9

"You're fucking crazy," said Noah.

"Are you going to help me, stop whining, or fuck off?"

"Fucking hell."

The two of them sat in the vents on the second floor at a grate overlooking the garbage shoot. Noah had spent two days showing Sam the building via the vents. Movement was hard and slow. "The garbage drops down to the basement, into commercial bins. They wheel them out once a week. It's the only way—apart from the stairs and the lift—down there. Vents stop here. No central air on the first floor, I guess. Or they botched the development," he pondered. "Look." He pointed along the corridor at head height. "CCTV cameras. They cover every corridor. Every. One."

Sam nodded. "I remember seeing cars parked over the entrance to the underneath car park."

"That's right. Keeps it locked down, I guess. But what good will being in the basement do? The entrance is shuttered."

Sam raised her eyebrows. "Yeah. Just formulating." She turned and started back towards the ladder that led to the next floor up, muttering something about Die Hard. As they climbed, she asked, "Tell me about the people here. I'm only seeing a few of them in the corridors."

"Yeah," whispered Noah from the ladder behind her. "It's like, there's Nanny, and her Prince's or General's, whatever, and a small arm of helpers. Thirty, forty? Aside from that there's the workers, and the women. Most everyone is related. Some of them are disabled. They're all fucking sick. When I was first in here, I got into one of the flats of one of the women. She was heavily preggo. I thought she'd be ideal to help me escape—I was sure she was here as a fucking baby machine." He laughed, climbing over to the next level and following Sam towards the next ladder. "She stabbed me in the fucking shoulder with a paring knife. A fucking *paring* knife."

"What did you do?" Sam got onto the next ladder.

"Punched her in the face."

Sam nodded. *Seems reasonable.* "I need to rest." She stopped at the next level and sat with her legs over the drop waiting for Noah. He joined her and sat with her. "I stink," she said.

"Yeah. Comes with the territory I'm afraid. There's squirt at home. Nicked it."

Sam smiled. "Squirt," she echoed. "Come on, then." She got up to her knees. "Let's go and get some squirt."

"Cheeky."

———

Sam watched silently from the vent grate. She was alone. Noah had been sleeping when she left. She was on twenty-four. It was the middle of the evening. She was chewing the sausage roll that she had recovered from the bin in one of the flats that was empty. It tasted like shit and she was wondering if that was because it was out of the bin or if it was vegan.

Nanny was sitting in the living room watching Eastenders.

Sam could just see her without opening the vent. She could see her arm and shoulder, the top of her head, from where she was sitting. She could see more of the TV and the sofa next to it, than Nanny herself.

She couldn't tell what room the vent opened into. It wasn't the bedroom, bathroom, or kitchen. Second bedroom, being used for storage, maybe? She turned her attention back to Nanny. *Cunt must die*, she thought. She stuffed her mouth with another bite of dodgy pastry avoiding the 'meat'. Even if it was a pork sausage roll the quantity of meat in it was probably negotiable.

The doorbell went. Sam tensed, stuffing the food into the satchel she had around her shoulder and pulling Noah's hunting knife out in its place.

Nanny got up and shambled out into the corridor, passing the doorway where Sam hid and going to the front door. Sam listened.

"Hello, come in," Nanny said.

There was a shuffling. Movement. Then Neil came into view. He was wearing a mock-leather jacket and jeans. A peak cap with NY written on it. Like this piss-ant had ever travelled further than fucking Tesco. He turned back to Nanny, still out of sight. He removed his hat like he was visiting the hospital, holding it to his chest.

"Come on," Nanny spoke again. She shuffled across toward the living room again. "Quick chat?" Nanny went to the chair she was sitting in and picked up the remote, muting the programme.

Neil joined her and sat on the sofa. He looked nervous. The confidence he had when he fronted Sam in the car park, that he had when … he fucked her mum's corpse … gone. He looked like a withered child. A boy.

"I'm sorry about what happened," Nanny continued.

Sam couldn't see Nanny as well as Neil. He nodded, caressing the peak of his cap. "S'all right," he said before he looked down.

"We need to sort it out though. The boy's are looking for the little whore. She will be found."

They're talking about me.

"Yeah. I know."

Nanny pushed herself up to her feet. She shuffled across to Neil and sat next to him, resting her hand on his knee. "You must be disappointed, but when she is found you can still have her."

This seemed to cheer him up. He smiled and nodded, looked back up. "Yeah," he nodded enthusiastically. "I was just ready, you know."

"I know," she said. "Why don't you stand up?"

Neil nodded and did as she suggested. He began to look nervous again.

Sam gripped the knife tighter, fixated.

Nanny reached around, using his hips to turn him to face her. She pulled his jeans open, struggling with fingers gnarled by arthritis, and yanked them to the floor. Neil rested his head back, looking to the ceiling as she pulled down his pants. "Look at me," she said. He obeyed.

She stroked his cock. Took it and squeezed. It flexed in her hand, twitching, getting harder.

"Nanny," he said.

"Calm," she replied. She started to stroke it properly. Wanking him like a fucking sixteen year old on the back seat of the bus.

"Nanny," he said, this time more urgently.

"You wait, you impatient little fuck."

They stared into each other's eyes.

"I'm gonna ..." he said.

"If you do," she said, letting the threat hang.

Neil grunted and spunk shot out over Nanny's hand and to the carpet in front of him.

"You wasteful cunt," she said, flicking it from her hand. She took a handkerchief and wiped herself with it. Then she slapped his balls. Hard. He flinched forward, and as he bent, she grabbed his ear like a scolding school teacher. She whispered something in his ear that Sam couldn't hear.

"Yes, Nanny." Neil pulled up his pants and his jeans, and then got to his knees. He put his hands behind his back and bent forward and started to lap up his cum from the carpet with his tongue.

Sam couldn't stop herself from making a wretch noise. It just came out. She slapped her hand over her mouth, holding her breath.

Neither of them seemed to notice.

She returned the knife to her satchel and felt the sausage roll. *Oh God.* She backed away from the grate and to the ladder. The last thing she needed to do was to alert them by puking.

CHAPTER 10

"So what's the plan?"

"A little bit of winging. I noticed yesterday that they've cleared our flat out. Again. Even took your blood soaked mattress this time. Fuckers. I nabbed a Stanley knife from where they were boxing things up." She took the knife from her back pocket and tossed it to the floor in front of Noah, still laying on his sleeping bag. "I've noticed that the bloke in eleven-oh-one is working odd shifts. The flat will be empty today, until about ten-thirty. Just out of interest, where did that blood come from on your mattress?"

"I got into a fist fight with one of Peter's boys the day I disappeared in here, and beat his brains in. You could say I was *venting*." He grinned at Sam.

She shook her head.

"Suit yourself." Noah looked at his watch, and shrugged. "So we only a few hours. What we doing?"

"I'm going to ransack his flat now."

Noah pulled himself up to sit. "You're fucking crazy."

Sam smiled. "Aye, so you keep telling me. You coming?"

"Do I have a choice?"

"Not if you want to have any fun."

Sam kicked the vent off in into eleven-oh-one's bedroom. The door was open into the hallway, and the place was empty.

"Careful," Noah hissed. He followed Sam out into the room and picked the vent from the carpet. "If it's too badly damaged, we won't be able to put it back. They'll know we've been here."

Sam shrugged. "By the time this fuck gets home from work they're already going to know." She went from the bedroom into the hall. One bedroom. She went into the bathroom and opened the cabinet above the sink and cleared a shelf into the sink with one hand.

"What are you looking for?" Noah was at the door, his voice an urgent whisper.

"I'll know when I see it." She glanced around the bathroom and then left, passing Noah and going to the kitchen. She lifted the satchel from her shoulder and placed it down on the kitchen counter top, flipping the lid open. She took the cleaver from the knife block and admired the blade. She placed it into the satchel. Then the chef's knife. She slid the paring knife from the base of the block and handed it to Noah, still watching.

He snorted. "Very funny."

She shot him a smile, and opened the cupboards under the sink. Bleach. She took it and handed it to Noah. "Hold on," he said. He bent down next to her.

"I don't know what your plan is for this, but ..." He placed the bleach back and picked up the drain cleaner. "This stuff is worse."

Sam nodded and took it from him, and the spray can of oven cleaner. "This stuff smells like shit. I wonder what it tastes like?"

"Gross," Noah stood. "What else?"

"This'll do for here."

"So now where?"

Sam smiled and pointed downwards.

They returned to the vents and went down three floors. It was hard work, but Noah was used to it and Sam was riding on adrenaline. Sam took Noah to the end of a vent. It led out into a living room on the eighth floor. The room was dirty. No one had cleaned for some time. There was a rug that looked gritty. The wallpaper was hanging off on the wall next to the armchair that faced the TV. Sam turned back to Noah and raised her finger to her lips. *Hush.* She carefully removed the vent grate, and crawled out into the room.

Noah followed her out and rested his hand on her arm, frowning at her.

She smiled a little. Only a little, but she gave a small tilt of the head to the side to signal that she knew what she was doing. She nodded for him to follow her.

They walked silently across the living room and to the entrance hall. It was a tiny square with four doors coming from it. Opposite them was the door to the corridor outside the flat. To the left was the kitchen. To the right was an open door to a bedroom, and from in there was the door to an ensuite toilet. The whole flat had a stale smell to it. Cigarettes and cheap booze. A strong lager smell.

As they reached the door to the bedroom the smell changed to a bodily stench. Sweat. Cum.

Sam walked into the bedroom first and stopped, still, at the end of the bed. She looked at Neil, sleeping. He was laying on his side, one knee up in the foetal position and the other our straight. Noah joined her, his eyes wide. He looked at her and raised his eyebrows. *Are we going to do this?* he was saying.

Sam nodded. Yes. Yes they were.

Sam pulled the chef's knife from the satchel and went to the head of the bed. She touched the point of the knife into Neil's cheek, pushing oh, so gently. He made a grumbly mumble and raised his hand to his face. She moved the knife so that he wouldn't feel it, and when his hand returned to next to him, he turned onto his back and let out a sigh.

Still his eyes remained closed.

His hand slipped into his pants, and he tugged on his cock.

Any joviality that was in Sam's face until now dropped and she took the knife and rested it, blade flat, on his mouth.

He opened his eyes and tensed to move.

"If you move," Sam said, "or make a sound, I will slit your throat."

He didn't move. Frozen. Paralysed in fear. His hand still on his cock.

She looked at his pants. "You were thinking of me?"

Neil looked around wildly. He was trying to find a way out. An escape. He looked at Noah stood at the end of the bed with some recognition. Noah smiled at him. "Well?" he asked.

Neil focussed back on Sam. He clearly didn't know what to answer for the best.

"Or were you thinking of my mum?"

His eyes widened.

"It had better have been me," she said. She lifted the knife from his face. "Well?"

Neil nodded. "Yes. You," he said. He still hadn't released his cock from his fist. He'd probably forgotten it was there.

Sam glanced back down to it. "Show me," she said.

Neil looked confused. His eyes flicked to Noah, who just shrugged.

She tapped the steel blade back down onto his face twice, impatiently. "Now."

Neil let his cock go, took his pants in his hand,

and pulled them down to free himself. He was at half-mast.

Sam smiled. "Is this shit actually turning you on?"

Neil let the edge of his mouth curl up.

"You fucking sicko." She stepped down the bed so she was at his waist. He watched her. She passed the knife to Noah. "If he moves, cut him."

Noah took the knife and went around the other side of the bed and towards his head, pointing the knife at Neil like he was preparing to fence. He looked a little confused as to what the plan was.

Sam sat. She took Neil's cock in her hand and gently stroked it. She felt him tense every muscle. "I can see you like that. Been waiting for me, I hear." Noah shot her a glance, but she ignored him. "Do you know what I like to do?"

Neil shook his head. He looked terrified, but had still managed to gain a hard cock.

"I like to be in charge." She smiled and let his cock go free. "Do you understand what that means?" She spoke to him like she was addressing a child.

He shook his head.

"It means I like to fuck men. You want me to do that?"

Neil looked at Noah who just stared at him. A blend of confusion and disgust sat on his face. Neil wasn't sure, but he managed a small nod. "How?" he whispered.

Sam grinned. "Ah, such an unaccomplished young man. You ever seen a woman with a dildo, fucking herself on a porn video?"

He nodded, a smile bursting onto his face.

"It's like that. But with your arse."

His eyebrow dipped as he processed what she was saying. Then he nodded slowly.

"So whatcha got?" She stood, giving his cock a gentle slap of encouragement. Over at the chest of drawers he had against one wall, she pulled the top drawer open. Porn mags. No surprise there. She looked in the next. Empty. The next, a smattering of unused hygiene products and some dirty clothes. Some rolling papers and a lighter. Tobacco and some weed. "Wow," she whispered, pocketing the lighter and the weed. "You really are a piece of work." She turned back to the room. "Not a lot there, is there?" She left Noah standing there over Neil with a hard cock. She made a mental note to thank him later, as this was probably more than a little uncomfortable for him. She went across to the kitchen and looked around. It was sparse. A couple of knives. Spoons. Forks. Plates, chipped. And everything was dirty. It smelled worse in here than in his bedroom. "Fuck's sake," she muttered.

She picked up an empty white cider bottle off the counter.

Walking back into the bedroom, the scene hadn't changed except Neil wasn't quite as excited. "Let's see what we can do," she said smiling. "Get onto your knees, face the wall."

Again, Neil looked unsure, but he obliged.

As soon as he was on all fours, naked, facing the wall, Noah mouthed to Sam, *What the fuck?* She winked at him. She came up on Neil and slapped him on the arse. "You know what a reach-around is?" She got on the bed behind him and grinded her pelvis against his arse, simulating fucking him, just like he'd done to her mum. She slapped his cock, as the fingers on her other hand teased his arsehole. She took the cider bottle and gently eased it into his arse. He let out a little whine. A whimper. But then he pushed back against it. He was enjoying it. She looked at Noah who was transfixed on the whole situation. He was staring at nothing like he'd checked out.

Sam clicked her fingers at him and waved for the knife.

He snapped back to her and passed it over. She smiled, easing the bottle out, and Neil made a noise like he had cum, then Sam lined up the chef's knife and pushed it to the hilt into his arsehole.

Neil's back arched, and he released a little grunt as if he didn't like what had just happened but didn't know if that was part of what was supposed to be happening.

Then he screamed.

"Shut him up," Noah blurted, bringing his hand back and laying a punch into the side of Neil's head.

Sam twisted the knife to the left and Neil stopped screaming. "You killed my mum, you ugly virgin cunt." She twisted it to the right.

Neil reached up and felt his stomach. He grunted and twisted, falling onto the bed. Sam let the knife go. He rolled onto his side, cradling his gut like he was going to puke. Blood started to piss from his cock, watery at first, then getting darker. She'd punctured his bladder with the knife.

"The fuck," Noah said. He looked at the door, as if he expected someone to burst through.

Sam looked at him. "He fucked my mum's gaping neck hole," she said, somewhat exasperated. "Did you think I was actually going to peg him?" She reached down and pushed Neil over, withdrawing the knife roughly. He coughed, and moaned, and blood started to come out of his mouth. Just a little. "Little bitch," she said. She grabbed his cock and held it. He wasn't in any shape to stop her. "Not so hard now, are you?" She laughed, letting him go. She rounded the bed and went to the head of it. She roughly rolled him onto his back. "Here," she said. "Suck this." She jammed the knife into his mouth.

He tried keeping his mouth shut, but she stabbed the blade into his teeth. "Take it." As his teeth chipped away, blood choking him, Sam could see that he was crying.

She stopped. "Baby."

The bed was soaked in blood now, coming from all of his orifices. Blood now gushed from his cock with no control.

She turned and stabbed the knife into his throat,

from the side. He froze. She pulled it out, blood now letting from there and not his mouth. Then she stuck it in again.

Noah and turned away, no longer interested in watching. He had his head in his hands.

Sam withdrew the knife again, and while Neil was still conscious, he had stopped moving, any fight he had left draining out onto the bed around him. She took the knife and started to hack at his neck. The blade sliding in with ease at first, slipping through the vocal cords and the larynx, above his Adam's apple. He stopped breathing when Sam broke through into the oesophagus. She started sawing as the blade hit the bones of the spine, but she found a gap in them, cutting down, through the spinal cord, and finally to the bedsheets. She pushed his head away and from the bed like a cat pissed off at a glass of wine. It landed on the carpet with a light plop.

"One down," she said. "Many to go."

And Noah puked on the carpet.

CHAPTER 11

"It stinks," Sam said, taking the next ladder up.

"I didn't mean too." Noah spat puke leftovers onto the floor of the vent as he followed.

Sam sighed. "Come on. Plenty more floors to go, and no time to waste."

They reach eighteen and stopped to rest. Sam dangled her feet over the side of the ladder and waited for Noah to catch her up. He'd been moving slowly, and she wasn't sure if it was the puke or the murder that had taken the wind from his sails. She kicked her legs back and forth mimicking her actions from when she was on the swing set in the old back garden. Better days.

She held her hand out and Noah took it, rising up and sitting next to her. It was a bit of a squash, the two of them together, but it worked. "What's next?" he asked, huffing.

"You okay?" she asked.

He nodded, waving his hand in front of his face.

"Nanny," Sam continued. "Cut the head off the snake."

"You think that's a good idea? It puts us a long way up."

She smiled and patted his knee. "Scared?"

"Nah." He laughed nervously as he spoke.

"Well, you should be." She let her hand rest on his leg gently. "It'll be fine. They won't find Neil for a while, it's still early."

"Give me five minutes, then," he said. He hung his head low while catching his breath, letting the thoughts of Neil fade. "So, as this appears to be the big push, so to speak …" he thought about how to finish the sentence.

"Well?"

He rested his hand on his arm, matching where her scars were. "We've been holed up together for a few days now, and I didn't know whether to ask or not."

Sam snorted. "Medical school," she said.

"They're not supposed to practice on you." He grinned, trying to lighten the mood, perhaps wishing he hadn't asked.

Sam shook her head. "First year student. I barely got through anatomy. Couldn't cope with the pressure, and this seemed to help." She ran her fingers across the lines she'd made with a razor blade. "Then dad pulled me out."

Noah rested his hand on hers. "What you gonna do when we get out of here?" he asked, changing the subject.

Sam stared down the vent. She hadn't even thought about it. She'd been in this vent system eating shit discarded by scum for a week, and all she had thought about was retribution. The look on her mum's face as she mouthed that she loved her was etched onto the back of eyelids and she saw it every time she closed her eyes. When she slept, she had nightmares about being forced to ask her dad to fuck her as he bled out on cheap carpet. What next?

"Go home," she said, suddenly. "Back to Camden. You?"

Noah shook his head. "Funny really. I've been in here so long that I don't know what I'd do with enough space to stand upright without looking over my shoulder."

"Come with me," she said, squeezing his leg. "We'll work it out together."

"Probably should contact my brother. No idea if he thinks I'm alive or dead." He looked at her, and then rested his head on her shoulder. "But together."

"Right then. Deal." She gently moved out from under him. "Come on then. Let's get this done."

The two of them started off again. Along the vent, and onto the next ladder going up.

Watching from the vent grate, Noah lay next to Sam. She was watching through, out into the flat. They could hear Nanny doing something in the kitchen and the TV was running to itself. Noah's focus was on the vent floor. "Have you been spending time here?" he asked, quietly.

Sam looked at him, then the vent floor. The crumbs from all the food she'd consumed, laying here, hour after hour, waiting. Watching. "A little. Pay attention." She turned back to look out of the vent.

"Now," he whispered. "I'm afraid to ask again, but do you have a plan?"

"For this one, I do. Wait for her to come back." She nodded at the TV. "Old cunt is making breakfast."

They waited. Sam was right, Nanny could be heard preparing food in one of the other rooms. The smell of toast drifted across the flat. Bacon. Coffee. It was driving Sam insane smelling it, and when she looked at Noah his face was contorted. "Patience," she said. "We will infiltrate and liberate the bacon."

"Coffee," he said. "Hot. Coffee."

"That too."

Nanny shuffled across the doorway carrying a disabled slip-proof tray in one hand. She rested it on the coffee table in front of the chair and sat down. She picked up the remote and turned the sound on the TV.

That was cue Sam was waiting for. She eased the vent open quietly, and crawled out, sliding the cleaver from her satchel in one silent movement. Noah followed.

"Heh." Nanny was engrossed in the TV.

The room was full of cardboard boxes. Storage. Sam quickly looked in the top of one of the open ones. Car stereos. The one next to it, toys. It looked like some Ebay empire. Fucking hell. Sam reached the door out into the hallway, looking to the right. The layout was different to the others she had been in yet again. Who had designed this fucking place? H. H. Holmes? There were two closed doors in the hall, one must be the bedroom and the other the bathroom. The door to the kitchen was open.

Sam crossed the hall to the living room doorway and waited while the sound from the TV lulled. As soon as the volume rose, she went in, followed by Noah. Sam crept up behind Nanny's chair, and looked at the top of her head. The temptation to take the cleaver and slam it into the top of her head was great, but not the plan. She glanced at the TV. Some morning cookery show. They announced an ad break and the screen went black for a few seconds.

Sam stared at the reflection of herself and Noah stood over Nanny while the screen was black.

Nanny looked at the screen in silence—able to see them just as clearly. "Well," she said quietly. "Look at what the cat dragged in."

Sam rounded the chair holding the cleaver up. "You keep your cunt mouth shut," she said to the old woman.

Nanny simply smiled. "As you wish."

"Now you give me one good reason not to kill you." Sam had no intention of walking away and leaving the old woman alive.

"I thought you wanted me to keep my cunt mouth shut?" She smiled, smugly.

Noah came around the side of the chair and

picked up a slice of bacon from the plate, untouched on the coffee table. He slipped it into his mouth. "Nice."

Nanny looked at him and smiled. It was a look of relief, as if she had just found the set of car keys she lost a week ago. "Hello, Noah," she said. "Looking good."

Noah chewed for a second and then picked up her coffee, carefully taking a sip, not used to the hot liquid. He picked up the butter knife from the plate and held it under her chin in the folds of the loose skin. "Lady asked a question," he said.

Nanny turned her smile to Sam. "Yes, she did. Didn't she? What was it? Why should you not kill me? Well." She thought for a second, and then pursed her lips, shaking her head. She looked up, brightly. "I can't think of a single one. You know, I've have a good innings, as they say. Cricket term, I believe. How do you want to do it? Cleaver, I see. Going to hack my head off? It's a little gauche, but it'll work." She started to pull herself from the armchair. "On the bed? It'll be easiest."

"Shut the fuck up." Sam pushed her back into the seat.

"Keep your voice down," whispered Noah. "These walls aren't that thick."

"No one heard us butchering Neil, did they?" Sam asked, returning the smug look that Nanny had given her.

Nanny looked down and gave a little look to the

side. "Oh well. He wasn't my favourite grandson."

Sam lowered the blade a little. "Your grandson?" her voice wavered.

Noah looked at her, sticking another piece of bacon into his mouth. "What's the problem?" he asked with his mouth full.

Sam felt her stomach tighten with nausea. "I saw her wank him off."

Noah's mouth dropped open. "*Fuuuuuuuck.*"

Nanny looked at him. "Oh no. I save that for my favourites."

Sam swallowed the vomit back. She hefted the cleaver up over her head and brought it down as hard as she could on Nanny's lower arm, just above the wrist of her hand, resting on the arm of the chair. The blade cut straight through the ulna and radius bones, cleaving it from the rest of the body. Nanny looked at it, stunned, for a moment, as her wrist and hand dropped from the arm of the chair onto the floor. "My wanking hand," she said. Blood spurted quickly from the arm and then turned to a dribble. The initial spurt landed on Noah's jeans. He turned and spat out his bacon.

"Fucking hell. This lot are worse than I thought."

Then Nanny screamed. It was a short, sharp, shrill shriek, that to be expected of a little old lady.

"She'll bleed out in a few minutes, if there's more than saw dust in her veins."

Then the door to the bedroom opened in the

hallway. Peter came out, naked apart from a towel around his waist. He was impressively cut for someone with the nickname *fat*. He looked at Sam and Noah, confusion turning to horror as he saw the blood on the carpet. And Nanny's wanking hand. Sam wondered for a moment what concerned him most, before slapping Noah's stomach as she took off toward the hallway, straight at Peter. She heard Noah follow and the two of them were in the hall and turning into the storeroom before Peter had time to react, stunned from the scene he had walked into.

Sam hooked into the storeroom and dropped to her knees, clambering into the opening of the vents. The last thing she wanted was to face off against someone who looked like they could snap her in half with one hand. She scrambled along into the vent and turned to pull Noah, finding he wasn't there. "Noah," she shouted, no longer concerned with stealth. A shadow became a face as Peter leaned down and looked into the vent.

"Noah's tied up. Why don't you come back and give him a hand?"

"Shit." Sam couldn't think. Instinct kicked in and flight won over fight. There was no way that she was going to be able to get out of the vent and stand a chance against Peter. He would mash her skull to powder before she gotten a blade to his skin. She was already on the ladder going down to the next floor, when she stopped. *Noah*. She climbed back up to twenty-four and clambered along to one of the small vents that opened out into the corridor outside the lift. She waited for what felt like an eternity before the lift *dinged*, and two men got out. They were in a hurry, leaving the lift and running to Nanny's front door.

Peter opened it, dressed now. Sam wondered if they all knew that Peter and Neil were both having fucking sexual relations with their grandmother. And also, how many of these other cunts were her grandkids? The two men went into the flat and returned, dragging Noah, unconscious, towards the lift. Peter slammed the door and followed them. The lift had gone, been called down to another floor, so they waited.

"That fucking bitch," Peter was saying. "She and this twat killed Nanny."

Good, Sam thought.

The goons with him paid lip service to their feelings, saying what a good old bird she was and how she would be missed. Then the lift arrived. They got in.

"Basement," Peter said. Then the doors closed.

At least he's still alive.

CHAPTER 12

Sam moved as quickly as she could. She was already tired, long before she had to hit the ladders, dropping down twenty or more floors. She got to two. The bottom of vent system. Made her way to the grate that overlooked the garbage shoot to the basement that Noah had shown her. Exhausted, she hoped that she wasn't too late.

She knew that this was going to be the last push. As soon as she left the vent here, she was going to be on CCTV for anyone watching. Maybe they wouldn't see her? Maybe they'd be doing something else.

Maybe they'd be in the basement with Noah.

Noah.

Sam swung her whole body around and raised her feet up to the grate. This vent came out at the top of the wall, not at ground level. It was going to make a noise. She kicked both feet against the grate, pushing it from the wall and to the floor. It crashed loudly when it landed, and Sam didn't even know if anyone was going to be standing there. She couldn't see much.

She pulled the cleaver. It was the blade with the most heft. Scooting forward, she pushed herself out of the vent and landed awkwardly on her feet, stumbling like a baby deer. She swung around half expecting someone to be charging at her. Nothing. No one.

She hurried over to the garbage shoot. Pushed the

flap open and looked down. It stank of rotten food. And she could hear noise. Noise of people coming from down there. She slipped the cleaver back into the satchel and raised herself up, lifting herself into the shoot, feet first.

"Here goes nothing," she whispered.

She left go and dropped down into the shoot. It was a sudden rush as she freefell for a second and then hit a slide, breaking her fall and slowing her for a couple more seconds, before she slid out of the shoot, into freefall again, and landed in one of the commercial wheelie bins in the basement. She sat stunned for a moment while becoming aware of her surroundings. She was in the trash, the walls of the bin high enough that she couldn't see out. At least that meant that they couldn't see her sitting there like a kid on the crapper. She could hear them, but the landing had left her numb, and with a strange underwater sensation to her hearing. Several? Lots? It was hard to tell. As the numbness subsided, she recovered her hearing as well, and the feeling of being underwater slowly cleared. There was pain in her upper leg. Near her gracilis muscle. She closed her eyes and hoped she hadn't broken her leg, or torn the muscle. That would probably sign her death warrant here and now.

She waited until she felt more like herself before looking.

There was a needle sticking out of her. A long one. "Fuck," she whispered. Needles didn't both her—never had—but having some dirty fucking addicts shit hanging out of her wasn't *exactly* ideal. She reached down and pulled it out carefully. She managed not to snap the needle off in her leg. It stung, probably infected already—she *was* sitting in almost literal shit—but fuck it. That was a problem for another day.

She wiped what she hoped was cold curry from her arm and crawled over to the edge of the bin, looking over the lip.

She was in the basement—it was where the stage was—where they'd ... to her mum. She backed away a little, and turned, leaning her back against the edge of the bin. She listened. There was commotion, but she could tell what was happening.

Pull your shit together, she thought, chiding herself. *That poor fucking guy risked his life to save you. What would it be like if he hadn't? Broken cunt and pregnant.* She nodded to herself. She went to the back of the bin, and climbed, out of sight of the crowd to the floor of the car park. She limped a little, trying to shake the fall and the needle out of her joints.

From the edge of the bin she could see more of what was going on, shrouded in the darkness, cover given by being in the far corner of the basement.

The stage stood against one wall. There was a crowd about it. Maybe ten of them? Again, it was all men. It was like some fucking boys club down here. Peter was on the stage. So was Noah. He was tied to a chair, just like her father had been. At least they hadn't stripped him. The stocks were still there, in the corner of it, cover by a bloody sheet. Sam hoped her mother wasn't still under there. *Surely not after all this time.*

Further away from her, on the opposite side of the basement—a wide expanse covering the footprint of the building, held up by reinforced concrete stanchions—was the shuttered exit. The height of the ceiling and wide enough for two cars to pass. The shutter was down, and Sam expected there was at least two cars parked on the outside of it.

It was hard to see the final wall—the one to her left and opposite the stage—there were stanchions in the way, but she could see the door to the stairwell and the lift in the far corner. There were a number of cars parked down here, surprisingly. They varied in age, but mostly seemed to be in storage. She saw their estate car in one of the spaces near the exit. She scrunched her face up wishing she had the keys for it.

She then looked back to Noah. He was starting to regain consciousness. He was looking around wide-eyed. He wasn't trying to get free, and Sam wondered if it was because he knew there wasn't any point, or if he was paralysed with fear. Maybe he was just thinking about how much better off he was before *she* turned up. She pulled the cleaver from the satchel and crossed to the safety of being behind a car. She looked around the garage. She needed something other than a cleaver to deal with at least ten of them.

There were enough cars that she could make her way around most of the garage without being seen. She started off in the direction of the lift. They didn't seem to be doing anything to Noah. *Yet.* Staying to the shadows as much as she could, she went along the wall. There were wooden pallets. From deliveries? She continued. Petrol cans. She lifted one. It had liquid in it. Probably siphoned off the cars after they'd been put down here to rot. Can't sell them, after all, not after you've inducted their owners into your incestuous tower block cult. She thought of her dad. *Or killed them.*

She continued around. There was an old security guard's office in the corner. It looked untouched since the eighties. The door was leaning against the wall next to it, and the small windowed office smelt of shit. There was a desk in there. A broken chair. The seat had been ripped off, making it look like a toilet. Maybe it was, judging by the smell. There was an old rotary phone of the desk. Sam crept in, staying low and picked up the receiver. There was a dial tone. She could end it now. She put her finger in the dial and twisted. It didn't move. Stuck together, glued? Rusted to fuck? Who knew? She replaced the receiver silently, and the phone gave off a little *ting*. She left the office. She was close to the stairs now.

The thought of fleeing crossed her mind again. Up the stairs and out the front door. Simple. But it wouldn't be, would it? Like the front door of the block would be open with them knowing she was on the loose.

She slid up on the side of a car and looked over to the stage. There was a little growing excitement, but she couldn't hear anything that was being said from here.

Then the door to the stairs opened and two young men came out. One of them screamed, *oi, oi, muthafucks*, his hands in the air. The two of them passed so close to Sam she could almost smell them.

They didn't see her. Their attention taken by the lit area surrounding the stage.

She watched them walk over, their *banter* being a mixture of taunts, insults, and camaraderie. Peter waved them on.

Sam stayed low and moved from car to car back the way she had come. She got to the petrol cans and started to quickly lift them. They all had something in them, from dribbles, to half full. She took two of them back to the lift and opened them. She sniffed the liquid to make absolutely sure it was petrol, before laying the two of them down, letting them leak over the floor. The petrol smelt strong. She wouldn't have long before anyone was alerted. And none at all, if someone else came out of the stairwell or the lift.

She went back, got two more, then went back to the first two cans, pouring more over the floor, creating a chain around the wall from the stairs back to the bins. When the last can lay emptying at her feet beneath the car in front of the bin, there was a sudden hush from the crowd.

She stopped. Held her breath. Had they heard her?

"Brothers," said Peter, standing at the front of the stage. The others had crowded around in a small semi-circle. "Nanny had left us." He dropped his head and put his hands together in remembrance. "She was a good lay." There was a hush over them. Some of them were looking around, horror on their faces at the surprise of her death, some with their heads bowed in respect. No one seemed surprised that Peter had been fucking her.

Well, thought Sam.

She took Neil's lighter from her pocket.

"And this piece of shit," Peter continued, "is responsible." He waved over to Noah. "Him and his little bitch."

Sam watched.

Peter walked over to the stocks and pulled the bloody cover from it. Thankfully they were empty. He dragged them into the middle of the stage. He was going to put Noah in them.

Sam rolled the spark wheel on the lighter. It was old, clunky, but it went round. No spark though.

Peter and one other roughly untied Noah. He struggled against them, but was no match for Peter's bulk alone, and not when he had help. They took him to the stocks and opened them forcing his head down into the centre hole and putting his wrists in the other two, clamping the wood down on him, trapping him.

They would kill him next, Sam thought, thumbing the wheel again. Nothing. "Fucking come on, you piece of shit," she whispered.

Peter came around to the front of Noah. He address the crowd. "What should we do with him?"

Kill him, came a voice. *Fuck him up,* came another. *Fuck him,* came the third.

Peter pointed into the crowd with one hand and touched his nose with the forefinger of his other hand. His undid his belt buckle and let it drop open.

CHAPTER 13

Peter stood on the stage, his trousers around his ankles. Sam now knew why he was called Fat Peter. Noah was staring at the man's flaccid cock in silent horror, his mouth wide open. Peter turned to Noah and pointed at the python between his own legs.

Sam could see Noah was crying, and this was revving the crowd up further. She tore her thumb down the spark wheel and the lighter fired. The flame launched upwards, almost taking her eyebrows off. "Fuck it," she muttered. She took a step back from the petrol all over the floor and tossed the lighter into it.

There was a loud pop as the vapour combusted before the flame reached the petrol, and then the blue and yellow flame rose. It wasn't large or impressive, but it moved quicker than Sam was expecting.

The flame flew across the floor of the basement, licking into the cars it passed, and illuminating the darkness in its wake.

It got Peter's attention quickly, as it reached the first of the laying down canisters, catching and exploding.

It wasn't like a Hollywood film—the room didn't shake. There wasn't a sudden wall of flame. There was a deafening crack that cut through the basement, as the canister was torn apart, and the petrol leapt up onto the cars and wall around it. Then the same happened to the next one.

Sam watched Peter scream and point, and suddenly everyone was rushing around in panic. Even Peter jumped down from the stage, sliding his massive dick back into his trousers, and running at the flames along with the rest of them.

Sam waited as long as she could, moving along the two cars toward Noah, finally breaking into a run at him when she felt Peter and his friends weren't going to look back at her. She ran like she'd never run before, ignoring the nagging pain in her leg from the needle. She pulled the chef's knife from the satchel as she did. She vaulted onto the stage and rounded Noah, jamming the knife into the edge of the wooden stocks, the handle vibrating in the air. She yanked the bolt of the stock towards her and pulled them open. Noah stumbled backwards falling onto his arse, his legs unable to take his weight. Sam gave a single glance back to the group, as she swung her hand in Noah's direction, hoping he'd take it and start to pull himself up.

They had been seen.

Noah took her hand and pulled himself up suddenly, almost dragging Sam off balance. She stamped her foot down to stay upright, and then Noah was there next to her. The two of them faced off against, maybe, a dozen of them. The two of them on the stage, and Peter and his group stood facing them, as the building behind them burned. The flames had taken a couple of the cars, the ceiling was filling with smoke.

Peter wrung his hands and shook his head. Then

he let out a subtle smile. He started to walk to them. The rest of his group walked behind him, acknowledging his leadership perhaps, or just fucking scared of the donkey dicked cunt. They got halfway between the fire and the stage before Peter waved them to a stop. "So what's the plan?" he shouted over the roar and crackle of the fire.

Sam shrugged. "Just winging it."

Peter nodded. The men weren't armed. Sam pulled the chef's knife from the stocks and stood firm. There was nowhere to run. They had to make a final stand.

Peter rolled his shoulders and snapped into a run.

Sam saw immediately that he was a fucking coward. He ran, his fists pumped, but he was achieving nothing more than a jog. He was letting his men, this brethren, his bitches, pass him to get into the fray first. "Good luck," she said to Noah.

"For your parents," he said.

Sam nodded, and pulled the cleaver from the satchel and handed it off to him. Then she turned and threw herself from the stage towards them.

CHAPTER 14

The two of Peter's quickest little bitches were a couple of younger lads. Sixteen, no more. Maybe younger. One of them was wearing a denim fucking tux, and the other a pair of shorts that were too small. Sam could see the angle they were taking. They weren't fighters. They were both running at her, unprepared.

Sam dropped to one knee as they got close, almost shoulder-to-shoulder. She would have said that they were probably brothers, but who wasn't here? She thrust the blade into denim tux's leg, just off the crotch. He screamed and tumbled passed her. She kept a firm grip on the blade and when the other was off balance, surprised by her attack, she slashed at him, belly level. There was contact, and he backed up, holding his large intestines in. She glanced at the one on the floor. He was cradling his leg and pissing blood like it was going out of fashion. She'd hit the femoral artery.

One look to Noah told another story. One of Peter's gang was on the floor, a cleaver impaled through his skull, into his right lobe. One of the others was tangling with Noah, hand-to-hand.

Sam was pushed hard backwards as something hit her across the face. She stumbled back and got her bearings. Another one. He'd punched her across the face. She looked at him, a little startled at first, and then pirouetted around towards Noah, sticking the guy he was tangling with. He rolled to the side, which gave Noah enough time to pull the cleaver from the stiff on the floor and take his own swing, slamming it into his jaw, crushing through the bone, seeing a fountain of blood spurt across all three of them.

"Thanks," he shouted. There was a noise behind him and he spun without thinking, cleaver back up like a samurai. Another went down.

Sam turned back to the one that he punched her. "*Cunt!*" she shouted and ran at him, launching herself into the air and landing on him like he was a gym horse. He went down under her force and as the two of them hit the floor, she let her weight push the knife through his chest plate, heart, pericardium, and left lung. He was dead before she was back to her feet. She looked over at Noah. He was bleeding from a wound on his temple. There was another, dead at his feet.

Noah looked her and they both looked around to Peter. He was looking around, wary, his army demolished. He was backing towards the wall of flames that now blocked the stairs and the lift. He shook his head, couldn't believe what he was seeing. Couldn't believe he was last man standing. *Last cunt standing.*

Sam looked down at herself. She was a shock of red. Blood from all of them. Noah had fared no better, except the blood on his face was his own.

They started towards Peter. He was choking. The smoke was starting to surround him. As they approached, he held his hands out like he was shepherding velociraptors. "Come on then," he said, goading them. "What are you waiting for?" He coughed more.

Sam span the knife around and reversed her grip. Noah had the cleaver. They surrounded him. Sam motioned in first, but faked to the side, and Peter dodged, Noah swung the cleaver, and Peter managed to knock it from his grip.

And Sam charged. She sliced his arm and butted her shoulder into him, knocking him from his feet. She pounced down onto him, landing one knee onto his chest, knocking the wind and the fight from him for a second. She held the blade to his throat.

"Do it," he wheezed. "Fucking do it, cunt."

"Get him up." She got off him. Noah held the retrieved cleaver to his neck and Sam kept the blade level on him. The smoke was thick now.

"What are you going to do? There's no way out. The longer you spend pricking around with me, the less chance you've got."

Sam smiled. "Come on," she shouted over the roar of the fire, waving him towards the stocks.

CHAPTER 15

Peter stood in the stocks, he made an occasional heave to try and open the thing, but they were made of stronger stuff than him. "You two will pay for this." The smoke had reached the stage now, the fire burning hard against the walls. Half the cars were on fire. The stairs blocked. The lift door burning.

Sam asked, "You and what army?"

Noah laughed, nervously. "We still gonna get out of here?"

"Hopefully," Sam said. She pulled the drain cleaner from the satchel. "What about this?"

Noah shook his head, covering his mouth with his arm, the acrid air stinking the basement out. "Nah," he said. "He'll never keep his mouth open. Pull his trousers down."

"What?" Peter blurted. "Fuck off." He started to buck against the stocks.

Sam shrugged and went around behind him, dropping his trousers and releasing the beast. Noah came around and joined her. He reached into the pocket of his hoodie and pulled out his paring knife. "Like it," Sam said.

"What?" Peter thrashed from side to side.

Noah started laughing and Sam went back to face Peter. She looked at the instructions on the bottle of drain cleaner. "One squirt or two?"

Peter didn't know what to do. He kept his mouth shut.

Sam took the cap off the bottle and leaned down to be at his level. "Will you remember my mum when you're drinking this? Open wide."

And Noah stabbed him in the dick.

Peter screamed and Sam squirted the liquid down his throat. When it hit the gag reflex he started to choke.

Noah came back around. "I lost the knife. It's kinda hanging outta his dick and I ain't getting close enough to retrieve it."

Peter was spitting up drain cleaner and cursing them out, blood forming in his mouth as the cleaner burned him like acid. He stopped when he saw his own blood start to pool under the stocks, weeping along the stage.

Sam looked at him closer. "Is he ... is he crying?" Then she laughed. "We need to get the fuck out of here."

Noah nodded in agreement.

They ran across the basement to the shutters that led to freedom. Padlocked closed. Sam ran over to her family's estate car. The keys were in the ignition. "Get out the way," she shouted to Noah, waving him over to the side of the shutters. She got in and slammed the car door, turning the key at the same time. She looked in the mirror as the engine turned over, seeing the wall of flames behind her. "Come on, you fuck ... piece of shit."

The engine started.

Sam slammed the car into gear and span the wheels, almost losing control as the back end spun out. Then the car lurched forward and hammered towards the shutters.

The car crashed into them, and the airbags failed as the car slammed to a stop, half in and half out of the basement. She couldn't see. Everything went black. "What the fuck," she said feeling around.

Then there was a hand on her. Pulling her from the car. "I'm blind," she said.

"Blood," said Noah, dragging her forward. "There's blood in your eyes. You hit your head."

She could see shapes and shadows and then brightness. Fresh air. The sound of the raging fire died down as they got further from the building.

They were out, into the car park.

Noah dragged her across the tarmac as she wiped the blood from her eyes, the two of them getting as far as the road opposite Tesco. The fire was burning up the outside of the building. The new cladding holding it in. Creating a funnel.

The skies burned red.

Sam saw that she'd punched a hole through the edge of the shutters, big enough for Noah to drag her through and out. She collapsed to the path and started to weep. Noah crouched down beside her. "The cops will be here soon."

Sam looked up at the building. The people

screaming at the windows. Women. Pregnant women. "This is going to take some explaining," she said.

About the Author

Ash is a British horror author. He resides in the south, in the Garden of England. He writes horror that is sometimes fantastical, sometimes grounded, but always deeply graphic, and black with humour.

Printed in Great Britain
by Amazon